H na Pielichaty (pronounced Pierre-li-hatty) h ritten numerous books for children, including *S. ne's Letters*, which was nominated for the C egie Medal, and the popular After School C series. A long-standing Huddersfield Town su orter, there are few who could write with as m n enthusiasm about girls' football. A local gi under 11s team helps with the inspiration ar tactical know-how, but Helena has been an vid fan of women's football for many years. It arly runs in the family: her aunt was in a women's team in the 1950s and her daughter has been playing since she was ten (she is now twenty-four!). Helena lives in Nottinghamshire with her husband and has two grown-up children.

The Girls FC series

Do Goalkeepers Wear Tiaras?

Can Ponies Take Penalties?

Are All Brothers Foul?

Is An Own Goal Bad?

Who Ate All The Pies?

What's Ukrainian For Football?

So What If I Hog The Ball?

Can't I Just Kick It?

Can't I Just Kick It?

Helena Pielichaty

WALKER
BOOKS

For all my friends at Forest Fields Primary School, Nottingham, but especially to Amritha Kaur, Hadia Sajjal, Mahfuza Parvin, Mujgana Hussainy, Sangeeta Kaur and Ms Sarah Rennie. Many thanks also to Karmjeet Kaur, for her good advice.

First published 2010 by Walker Books Ltd
87 Vauxhall Walk, London SE11 5HJ

10 9 8 7 6 5 4 3 2 1

This book has been typeset in Helvetica and Handwriter

Printed and bound in Great Britain by Clays Ltd, St Ives plc

British Library Cataloguing in Publication Data:
a catalogue record for this book is available from the British Library

ISBN 978-1-4063-1740-4

www.walker.co.uk

☆☆ The Team ☆☆

☆ **Megan "Meggo" Fawcett** GOAL

☆ **Petra "Wardy" Ward** DEFENCE

☆ **Lucy "Goose" Skidmore** DEFENCE

☆ **Dylan "Dyl" or "Psycho 1" McNeil** LEFT WING

☆ **Holly "Hols" or "Wonder" Woolcock** DEFENCE

☆ **Veronika "Nika" Kozak** MIDFIELD

☆ **Jenny-Jane "JJ" or "Hoggy" Bayliss** MIDFIELD

☆ **Gemma "Hursty" or "Mod" Hurst** MIDFIELD

☆ **Eve "Akka" Akboh** STRIKER

☆ **Tabinda "Tabby" or "Tabs" Shah** STRIKER/MIDFIELD

☆ **Daisy "Dayz" or "Psycho 2" McNeil** RIGHT WING

☆ **Amy "Minto" or "Lil Posh" Minter** VARIOUS

Official name: Parrs Under 11s, also known as the Parsnips

Ground: Lornton FC, Low Road, Lornton

Capacity: 500

Affiliated to: the Nettie Honeyball Women's League junior division

Sponsors: Sweet Peas Garden Centre, Mowborough

Club colours: red and white; red shirts with white sleeves, white shorts, red socks with white trim

Coach: Hannah Preston

Assistant coach: Katie Regan

☆☆ Star Player ☆☆

☆ **Age:** 9½

☆ **Birthday:** 7 May

☆ **School:** Mowborough Primary School

☆ **Position in team:** mainly midfield

☆ **Likes:** mendhi parties, hanging out with friends, school

☆ **Dislikes:** Dad doing stuff without telling me

☆ **Supports:** Liverpool

☆ **Favourite player(s) on team:** Megan and Petra

☆ **Best football moment:** when Megan got the team together

Tabinda "Tabs" Shah

☆ **Match preparation:** I try to do breathing exercises and warm up properly

☆ **Have you got a lucky mascot or a ritual you have to do before or after a match?** Not really. I'm too busy trying not to be ill! I get quite nervous.

☆ **What do you do in your spare time?** I help Mum and Dad in the garden centre, watch TV or play on the Wii with my cousins.

☆ **Favourite book(s):** **Chips, Beans and Limousines** by Leila Rasheed

☆ **Favourite band(s):** JLS

☆ **Favourite film(s):** Up

☆ **Favourite TV programme(s):** Jinx

Pre-match Interview

Hello. My name is Tabinda Shah. I'm in Year Five and I play midfield for the Parrs U11s. My dad's family are from Gujarat in India and my mum's are from the Punjab in India, but I'm from Mowborough in England!

I am going to write about the early part of the season. We've played four games and have somehow found ourselves at the top of the table, but as our coach, Hannah, keeps telling us, we mustn't let it go to our heads. It's funny she should say that, as you are about to find out…

Anyway, here's the table. Go Parrs!

Your friend,
Tabinda

The Nettie Honeyball Women's Football League junior division

Team	P	W	D	L	Pts
Furnston Diamonds	4	3	1	0	10
Grove Belles	4	3	1	0	10
Parrs U11s	4	3	1	0	10
Tembridge Vixens	4	2	2	0	8
Greenbow United Girls	4	1	1	2	4
Cuddlethorpe Tigers	4	1	0	3	3
Hixton Lees Juniors	4	1	0	3	3
Lutton Ash Angels	4	1	0	3	3
Southfields Athletic	4	1	0	3	3
Misslecott Goldstars	4	1	0	3	3

1

It was a wet Saturday morning in late October and we had won a corner against Lutton Ash Angels, the dirtiest team in the league.

"Tabs! Get in there to help," Hannah shouted from the touchline.

Reluctantly I left the safety of an empty midfield and jogged towards the goal area. My heart began thudding in my chest. I didn't like it over there. It was too busy. Too cramped – even Megan had raced from her goal to lend support. The Lutton Ash defenders loomed above me like skyscrapers, blocking my view. I couldn't see a thing, and it wasn't until someone called out "Incoming!" that I even knew we had taken the corner.

"Mine," Shell, the Angel with the nasty hair-pulling

habit, declared. I shrank back, hoping Gemma would do her usual wonderstuff and nod it in, but Megan turned to me, rain dripping down her face. "Jump for this one. It's got your name on it," she ordered.

"OK," I said, my voice coming out in a tiny squeak.

As if by magic, the towering defence parted, and there was the ball, zooming like a rocket straight towards me. My skin prickled with sweat.

"Jump!" Megan repeated. "Jump, or you are out of the team."

I'd already had several warnings about my bad attitude. Shocked, I screwed up my eyes, steeled myself and jumped. But nothing happened. Some invisible force was holding me down. I tried again, but exactly the same thing happened. I couldn't move.

Just then a familiar voice said, "Tabinda! For goodness sake!"

I blinked. My reflection in the mirror blinked too

as my daydream evaporated and Mum removed her hand from my shoulder. She wagged the hairbrush at me. "Don't fidget. I haven't finished getting all the lugs out yet."

"Sorry," I said.

She returned to the rhythmic brush strokes that had sent me into a stupor, but I kept my eyes wide open this time. It was bad enough that I'd be playing Lutton Ash for real in two hours; I didn't need my worst fears to grip me now. What I needed was a distraction. Quick. "Is my hair as long as yours was when you were my age?" I asked.

"Nope. I could sit on mine," Mum said with an extra hard pull that made me yelp.

"Ouch! Mum! Pull much harder and my eyes will shoot out."

"As if."

"I'm not even kidding. My eyes will shoot straight from my head into the wall, then bounce off and roll about on the floor like bloodstained marbles.

They'll roll and roll, getting grittier and grittier and dirtier and dirtier. Then when I put them back in, I'll only be able to see crumbs and bits of hair. People will call me Yeti Eyes for the rest of my life."

Mum stopped brushing. "What on earth are you talking about?"

"Nothing. I'm just rambling to take my mind off something."

"Let me guess. Bloodstained marbles. Yeti eyes. That something wouldn't be the Halloween party, would it?" She reached over my head to the wicker basket on the windowsill and swapped the brush for the long-tailed metal comb. A second later her silver bracelets began clacking against each other as she started to carve – I mean, *divide* – my hair into three sections.

"Not exactly," I told her.

She smiled, not believing me. "Remind me again how we got lumbered with hosting a Halloween party in the garden centre?"

"It's not a Halloween party. It's a team-building

exercise that happens to fall on Halloween," I corrected.

"Remind me again how come we got lumbered with hosting a team-building exercise that happens to fall on Halloween in the garden centre?" she repeated.

"Because the function room at the club was already booked and Dad offered. And it's not the whole garden centre, just the grotto."

"Hmm. The same grotto that's due to be full of artificial Christmas trees any day. And did Dad offer to clear that grotto up afterwards?"

"We'll clear away," I told her as she began the plaiting proper. "It's part of the whole team-building thing. We dress up. We bring food. We have fun. We clear away afterwards."

"I'll believe that when I see it."

"See what?" Dad asked, emerging from the kitchen and putting Mum's coffee down on the windowsill.

"We're talking about next week," I told him.

"Can't we just focus on this week first? Like hurrying up with the hair stuff."

Mum rounded on him. "Excuse me. For your information, the 'hair stuff', as you call it, is a vital part of the pre-match preparation. Isn't that right, Tabinda?"

Mum looked at me, waiting confirmation.

"Absolutely," I told her.

"See." She sniffed. "And even though she will end up looking as if she's crawled through a hedge backwards by the time she gets home, I like to think I've made some small contribution to her footballing career."

Dad sipped his coffee. "Fine, fine. Whatever you say. Just *hairy* up," he said, making me and Mum groan.

2

If Mum's pre-match preparation was plaiting my hair, Dad's was doing my head in. "So how many goals are you going to score today, Binda?" he asked, reversing down the long drive that separates our house from the garden centre. "Sixteen? Seventeen?"

"Seventeen? So likely!"

"I'll settle for two, then."

"I'll settle for just surviving," I mumbled as we joined the main road.

Dad frowned. "There you go again. Being negative. I was exaggerating with sixteen, but two is not beyond you. Two is *do-able*."

I took a deep breath, hoping Dad wasn't going to start putting pressure on me. I was anxious enough, and my stomach was already beginning to churn.

"You know your problem on that team?" he asked.

"No, Dad." I sighed.

"You are over keen to pass the ball."

"I kind of thought that was the idea."

"Yes, yes – but there are times when you look as if you can't wait to get rid of it. You need to assert yourself more. Run with it. Dribble with it."

"Uh-uh," I said, wrapping my arms round my tummy as we passed the sign for Lutton Ash. Only another three miles. Three short little miles and less than sixty tiny minutes to kick-off.

"And when you are in the area, don't automatically set it up for one of the others. Make your presence felt. Have a shot. If you miss, you miss..."

Sweat prickled my forehead. "Yes, Dad."

"Relax more on the ball..."

I stopped listening. I couldn't take anything in any more. My stomach was really aching now. Unlike Megan, who's famous for being tense on match days, my nerves don't disappear once the whistle goes. My butterflies grow and grow during the match until they're as huge as Queen Alexandra's Birdwings, the largest species of butterfly on the planet. I get so bad that there are times when I think I'll throw up on the pitch. In fact, I did throw up once – when we were playing Lutton Ash Angels, funnily enough.

Do you want to know why I get so tense? It's in case I have to do a header. Yep. A header. That daydream I had while Mum was brushing my hair wasn't random. Being forced to head the ball really is my worst-case scenario.

Don't ask me why. I know they're easy. I know they don't hurt. I know they're part of the game. It's just that when I see the ball hurtling towards me at head height something snaps and I panic. I'd rather be chucked in a bath full of rats any day than do a header.

I haven't told anyone about it – especially not my dad. He'd be on the phone to Hannah like a shot, asking her to give me individual coaching as a "small favour", or something as equally embarrassing. He thinks that because he sponsors the team he can ask for special treatment. He's always doing it. I overhear him sometimes: "Oh, and, Hannah, before I hang up, I just wondered if you'd thought about playing Binda out wide on Saturday? I think that's her natural position..." Or "Perhaps Binda could *start* the match tomorrow, rather than coming on later?" It makes me die.

I'm sure Hannah thinks I'm a total spoilt brat. I know for a fact Jenny-Jane does. I hate it. I do not want to be singled out because my dad pays for stuff. I'd rather just hang out in the background, with my sad little secret, thank you very much.

Besides, I've managed OK so far. If a high ball comes towards me in open play, I make sure I back-pedal so fast that it's chest height by the time it reaches me. Or I pretend to go for it and accidentally-on-purpose kind of miss and let it sail over my head. There's no reason why I can't just carry on like that for a few more months – or years – is there? I do enjoy playing otherwise, and it's not as if I'm useless. Hannah and Katie often shout "Good feet! Good feet, Tabs!" when I've got possession. *Good feet.* That's what matters, isn't it? The game is called *foot*ball, after all.

3

Hannah was telling Jenny-Jane off when I joined them. "I don't care what you think, JJ," she was saying to her, "it looks silly."

Reluctantly Jenny-Jane pulled her black shorts lower so the waistband wasn't under her armpits. "Stupid pink shirt," she muttered.

I pretended not to hear and darted quickly past. That stupid pink shirt was another reason I was trying to keep a low profile. Dad had chosen it. I'd told him that just because it was the colour of *his* favourite sweet pea didn't mean it would be popular with everyone else. Had he listened to me? No. Had I been the one to get it in the neck at the start of the season from JJ and one or two others? Yes. Cheers, Dad. That helped me fit right in.

"Morning, Tabs," Katie said, making me jump.

"Morning."

"All right?"

Not really, I wanted to say. I feel lousy. I feel sick. I feel scared. "Yes, great thanks," I said instead.

To warm up, we all set off in a huddle across the wet and soggy grass. It was always miserable weather when we played this lot. It was like an omen or something.

As everyone chatted, I tried to concentrate on gently breathing in and out to settle my nerves, but the conversation kept coming back to the Halloween party and therefore to me.

"Is it OK to bring sausage rolls?" Lucy wanted to know.

"Sure," I said.

"Only Mum asked me to ask you. She thought it might be rude to bring them, with you not eating meat."

"We don't eat *much* meat at home, but the

party's in the grotto, so it's no problem. We serve ham paninis and things in the cafe."

"Cool."

Holly was next. "Will there be a sharp knife to cut cake?"

"I can ask."

"Tracie and me are baking a Halloween cake we found in a magazine. It's got this special gungy black icing that takes ages to mix, and dozens of sparklers."

"Sounds lush."

"Oh, by the way, we'll need matches to light the sparklers."

"Matches. Right."

"How dark will it be?" Amy then asked.

"What? The cake?"

"No, the grotto. I need it to be uber dark for my costume to work."

"I'm not sure. I'll have to check with Dad."

"OK. But remember, *uber* dark if you get a choice."

"Uber dark. Got it." I nodded.

"What are you coming as?" Nika wanted to know.

"I could tell you" – Amy smiled, tapping the side of her nose – "but then I'd have to kill you. It is brilliant, though. Mum ordered it online from America."

"We're coming as skelebones," Daisy and Dylan chimed in from behind me. "Darwin's spent hours cutting our ribs out."

Sausage rolls. Gungy icing. Rib-cutting. None of this was helping my stomach much.

"The pitch will be heavy and slippery today," Hannah told us after we'd been through our warm-up routine and drills. "So be careful. Amy and Hols, I'll have you at the back for starters. Mark up well, but steer clear of any fifty-fifty tackles. I don't want any injuries – especially as we've got the Grove Belles next week..."

"And the Halloween party," Dylan chipped in. "We're coming as skelebones."

"And the Halloween party," Hannah said with a roll of her eyes. "Nika, Gem and Tabs, I'll have you three in the middle, with Eve up front. OK?"

I was in the starting line-up. Dad would be really pleased. My stomach wasn't so sure. Inside it, the Queen Alexandra butterflies – or Queenies, for short – were rehearsing for *Strictly Come Dancing*. They kept swapping from the jive to salsa and back again.

"Play the ball forward as much as you can," Hannah continued, looking at me, Nika and Gemma, "but don't take any risks if they come at you. We don't want any accidents."

"What if they foul us?" Amy asked.

"Keep calm and carry on. Play to the whistle."

"But the referee's that Shell's dad!" Holly said.

We all turned. Sure enough, the ref was giving his daughter a quick hug before marching across to the centre spot. He caught us staring at him and tapped his wrist as if to say, "Look sharp."

"Play to the whistle," Hannah repeated.

As we took up our positions, Megan's mum yelled, "Come on, you Parsnips!" at the top of her voice. Then the skies really opened – before Shell's dad had taken the whistle from his lips, the rain was bouncing off my hair and dripping down my nose. It *was* an omen. I could feel it in my skelebones.

4

Despite my bad feeling we were 5–0 up by half-time. Lutton Ash just couldn't put two passes together and spent more time shouting at each other than playing football.

During the break, the rain stopped and the sun broke through the clouds. I felt a little more cheerful as Hannah swapped us round. I was put on for Gemma in central midfield. Yikes! I was nowhere near as good as Gemma, but I suppose Hannah thought she could risk it with us being so far ahead. Dad – who always liked to eavesdrop on the half-time talk – leaned over and whispered in my ear, "Use it as an opportunity to show what you can do."

"Yes, Dad." I sighed.

Actually it was Shell who used it as an opportunity to show what she could do – like foul a lot. Within seconds, Daisy was sprawled out on the grass. Daisy being Daisy bounced straight back up again. The ref didn't blow for a foul, of course, and Shell ploughed on.

I ran back to defend, marking up a blonde-haired girl who kept shouting, "To me! To me!" Shell ignored her and hoofed the ball upfield to no one in particular, where it struck Holly on the arm. The whistle blew immediately. "Hand ball. Free kick," Shell's dad announced.

Holly opened her mouth, but before she could protest, Shell had decided that she was going to take the free kick and placed the ball about three metres closer to the goal than it should have been. Everyone apart from Eve piled into the area. I followed the blonde girl to the left-hand post. I was trembling. The Queenies were at full pelt now. This was exactly the kind of situation they loved and I dreaded. Free kicks usually came in high and cried out for a header, one way or another: into the goalmouth from an attacker or out to safety by a defender. I did not want to be that defender.

As Shell kicked, my stomach began to heave and instead of marking up and defending the post, I darted forward, away from the huddle and into space.

At the same time – by some fluke – Shell's feeble free kick landed right at my feet, and because I had been running forward, I just kept going. I ran with the ball as fast as I could, half expecting to be tackled any second – but I was so far ahead nobody caught me. I then squared it to Eve, who simply ran the last few metres to the goal, had a brief one-on-one with their unprepared keeper and scored!

"Wahoo!" I heard my dad cheer.

Lutton Ash fell to pieces after that and spent most of the time barging each other out of the way instead of us. Shell's dad even had to blow the whistle once, when the blonde girl snatched the ball out of Shell's hand after she'd tried to take another "free kick". "Give someone else a chance! You always mess up!" she'd snapped.

"I'll mess you up!" Shell retorted before taking the free kick – and messing it up.

The match ended 7–0 in the end. When Megan shouted, "Three cheers for Lutton Ash," we all bellowed, "Hip-hip-hooray!" as loud as we could.

The Queenies had packed up, and I left the pitch feeling brilliant. We'd won and I'd been wrong about omens. Nothing bad had happened at all.

After we'd warmed down, Hannah and Katie gathered us round for the post-match briefing.

"That was wicked," Hannah told us. "You ignored all provocations and just dug in. It's like my nan always says: 'Cream rises to the top.'"

"We are top! Top of the league!" Megan grinned.

That set some of them off chanting, "We are top of the league! We are top of the league!"

"Don't get carried away, girls," Katie warned. "We've got the Belles next week!"

The chant instantly changed to, "We *were* top of the league! We *were* top of the league," making us all laugh.

"OK," Hannah announced when we'd calmed down. "On to today's Player of the Match..."

"Let's give it to Smelly Shell!" Eve joked.

"No way." Hannah laughed. "For sheer brilliance, today's Player of the Match goes to ... Tabinda the tenacious!"

I stood there blinking as everyone clapped. I was delighted but a bit bewildered. Why had I won it? I hadn't scored. I hadn't had *that* much possession. Even Hannah's explanation didn't make sense. "The way you turned defence into attack after the Angels' free kick was genius. And to set Eve up to score on top of that – double genius! Well done you."

I blinked a few more times as she pressed the trophy into my hand. I'd done what? I thought as the rain began to fall again.

5

Dad was beside himself on the journey home. "Player of the Match! I knew it would happen one day. I'm so proud. So proud." I looked at him. I actually thought he might cry. "Turning defence into attack? Is that what Hannah said? And you did. You did! Holly's dad and I saw it. The move took us both by surprise."

"It took *me* by surprise. Dad, I—"

"That showed real maturity as a player. Way above average for that level. I knew it was only a matter of time before your confidence improved. I just knew it."

"Dad..." I began, but he gone into his dream world.

"That's decided me. First thing Monday, I'm going to find out who runs the nearest centre of excellence and phone them…"

My stomach lurched like a car doing an emergency stop. "Centre of excellence? Dad, no. I'm not good enough. And even if I were, I wouldn't go. I like playing for the Parrs. They're my friends..."

"Binda, darling, I hate to break it to you but you're not going to be a Parr for ever. Half the team will be ineligible for the Under Elevens by summer. Then what?"

"We'll become Under Twelves," I said.

"No, no, no. It's all going to change. Trust me on this one."

"It's not," I said. I didn't want it to change. I liked it as it was.

"Of course it is. We've got to look to the future."

I was beginning to feel really muddled. How had we gone from me winning the Player of the Match trophy to the team collapsing?

Dad carried on, oblivious. "Ha! Wait until they see my Binda out there at Wembley representing England in a few years' time. Eh?"

What? Wembley? This was nuts! Dad was really worrying me now. I'd never seen him this excited. "Dad. You're being mental."

He frowned. "Why?"

"Wembley. As if!"

"OK, you're right. One step at a time."

"Thank you."

"You'll need to go through a centre of excellence first. I wonder where the nearest one is. Leicester probably. Maybe Derby, or Birmingham. I wonder if they need a sponsor..."

Unbelievable! I leaned forward and switched on the radio. Lady Gaga blasted out. "Mam-ma-mam-ma-ma ... ma ... poker face..."

"What's that rubbish?" Dad asked.

Better rubbish than you talking, I thought, and turned the volume higher.

6

Lady Gaga's singing must have done the trick because Dad didn't mention the centre of excellence thing again all weekend. I guess it could also have been because I hardly saw him. He had to work on Sunday and I had to go with Mum to the gurdwara, so it was after five before we all sat down together. Then by the time Mum had filled him in on all the news about her sisters (Auntie Amritha and Auntie Sangeeta), and I'd told him all about what I'd learned in Punjabi class, there wasn't much time left to talk about centres of anything. He did try at one point, asking where my Player of the Match trophy was, but Mum rescued me by interrupting with a question of her own. "Never mind trophies," she said, "what about this party?"

"What about it?" Dad asked.

"Well, what's happening? What do I need to do for it? You must tell me now, so I can plan ahead. Otherwise you know what will happen – the week will fly by and people will turn up and nothing will be ready."

Dad shrugged. "You don't have to do anything, Karmjeet. This is Parrs' business, not Sweet Peas'."

Mum coughed. "Excuse me, buddy, but seeing as the party is taking place in *our* garden centre, I think it is my business."

"People *have* been asking things," I said, backing Mum up.

Dad frowned. "Such as?"

"Well, Holly needs a knife and matches..."

"What?" Mum gasped.

"For the cake," I reassured her, laughing at the look of surprise on her face.

"Phew!" Mum said, her hand on her chest as if she was having palpitations. "You had me going there. I know some people take Halloween very seriously…"

I grinned, happy now that the conversation was fully on the party and not on football. "Amy is the one doing that," I told Mum. "She needs the grotto to be uber dark."

Dad looked puzzled. "Uber dark?"

"As in pitch-black."

"No problem." He shrugged.

Mum rolled her eyes. "No problem, he says. No – no problem at all, apart from the fact that Fun Forests are delivering all the Christmas stock tomorrow and we have nowhere to put it. There's also the small matter of a dozen girls eating food in the grotto and leaving crumbs everywhere for mice to find…"

"Mice? What mice?" Dad wanted to know. "We don't have mice. Unless you count the sugar ones in the gift shop."

"Food will have to be eaten in the cafe," Mum said decisively.

"OK," Dad agreed, rapidly realizing that this was one Parrs event he wasn't going to have total control over. "Food in the cafe."

"We can lay on coffee and cake for parents, too."

"Parents?" Dad and I both asked.

Mum stared at us in amazement, as if she couldn't believe what she was hearing from the two nitwits in front of her. "Well, you can't expect them to sit in the car park for two hours!"

"We don't want parents around. They'll get in the way," I grumbled.

Mum looked thoughtful. "They could always browse the gift shop. I don't mind keeping it open."

"That's a good idea," Dad agreed immediately. "We could offer them a special Parrs discount. Fifteen per cent off everything."

"Trust you, Ali!" Mum protested.

"What?"

"To use it as a business opportunity."

"What's wrong with that?"

"Why can't we keep the party as a chance to mingle?"

"For sure." Dad smiled, his eyes lighting up. "A chance to mingle with an option to purchase."

"No," Mum said, "what I meant was that *I'd* like to mingle."

"You?"

"Yes. Me. How many times have I seen Binda play? None – because I am always working."

"We could always swap," Dad offered.

"That's not what I'm saying," Mum told him. "It's just that I've heard so much about these girls and their parents, I'd like to meet them."

"Well, of course you must," Dad soothed. "It will be a good opportunity. You're much better on the charm offensive than I am." He then started talking about wheeling a trolley of winter pansies and dwarf heathers into the shop entrance on the night.

Mum and I exchanged glances. Typical Dad. Once he got an idea in his head, nothing stopped him. He toddled off to find a notepad to start a “to do” list. I went to bed happy, feeling confident that the only centre of excellence occupying Dad was the one called Sweet Peas!

7

It wasn't until training on Tuesday that my football fears started up again. Sometimes Hannah discusses the previous match to make a point, and I had convinced myself that she would call me out to demonstrate my "amazing" move. Every time either she or Katie stopped us all to teach a point I looked down at my trainers, my heart pounding, in case this was The Moment.

It came right at the end. "Good work, girls, good work," Hannah told us, her voice echoing around the sports hall. "If you play like that during the game on Saturday – keeping passes simple – you'll be a pleasure to watch."

Then she turned to me.

Uh-oh, I thought. Here it comes.

"Tabs."

"Yes?" I gulped.

"Don't look so worried, I'm not going to bite. I just wanted to check if there was anything we need to know about the Halloween party afterwards? Your dad sent me a text about us now eating in the cafe, or something?"

I sighed with relief. "Yes. And Mum says to tell you that parents are welcome to stay. She'll provide refreshments for them and they can look round the gift shop if they want."

Everyone began to chat at once.

"Are you serious? A party *and* shopping at the same time? How perfect a night out is that?" Amy gushed.

Megan groaned.

"What's up, Meggo?" Katie asked.

"Well, no one's going to be focused on the Belles match now, are they? Now you've mentioned the 's' word."

My heart leapt. Although Megan had directed her comment at Amy, I felt personally responsible for this new problem. Now if we lost it would be my family's fault for distracting everyone with thoughts of scented candles and potpourri. It was the pink strip all over again. Luckily, Hannah dealt with it in a beat. "Right. Listen up, people. For the sake of Megan's sanity, all talk of witches, vampires and gift shops is banned until *after* the Belles game. OK?"

"OK," everyone agreed.

Hannah turned to Amy, to double-check she understood. "Amy?"

"I know," Amy said, briefly looking up from filing her nails. "Chill, babe!"

Everyone laughed then, and Hannah rolled her eyes. "Well, 'babes', I'll see you all Saturday. Quarter to ten sharp at the club."

I was still smiling about Amy calling Hannah a babe when Dad picked me up.

"You look happy," he said.

"I am."

"So you should – a girl with your talent."

"What talent?"

"*What talent?* That's my girl, so modest. Your emerging footballing talent, of course."

Not again! "Don't even go there, Dad," I told him. "That's not why I'm smiling."

"You wait until Saturday. You'll be really smiling then."

That sounded fishy. I looked at him. "What do you mean?"

"Nothing."

He said "nothing" far too cheerily for my liking. "You didn't do anything dumb, did you?"

"Dumb? Such as?"

"You know, like phone-some-centre-of-excellence dumb."

"What? No, no, of course I didn't. When would I have had the time?"

"Please promise me you haven't," I said.

"Goodness me, Binda. Don't get so worked up about things. You're as bad as your mother for flapping over trivialities."

"I just don't want anything to do with centres of excellence, OK?"

"OK! OK! I get it. Let's change the subject."

"Good idea."

"Did I tell you that I found a perfect place for the artificial trees?"

"No."

"They are going to become a spooky forest leading to the grotto."

"That's brilliant," I told him, genuinely impressed.

"I'm not just a pretty face, you know." He grinned.

I felt really bad then for jumping to conclusions. Both my mum and dad worked really hard; they didn't have to use up all their spare time doing these extra things for me and the team. "I'm sorry, Dad. I didn't mean to whinge," I said.

"And I didn't mean to tease," he said. "Let's just concentrate on the party for the rest of the week, huh?"

That was fine by me.

8

We did just that. Every afternoon, straight from school, I'd go and help Dad transform the grotto from what was basically a dumping ground into a Halloween spectacular. By Wednesday, all the artificial Christmas trees had been arranged in two rows on either side of the entrance and draped in cobwebby mesh, while, inside, everything had been cleared out, apart from piles of cushions for us to sit on. Around the walls giant toy spiders, luminous skulls and rubber bats dangled from sections of freestanding garden trellis. It was all looking good.

On Thursday a grey metal contraption, about the size of a rabbit hutch, appeared. "What's that?" I asked.

Dad grinned and pressed a switch. Cold white mist immediately poured out of a nozzle at the front and spread rapidly along the floor, clamping at my ankles.

"A fog machine! That's wicked, Dad!" I yelled.

Mum had been doing her bit, too. She had spent hours blacking out the windows in the cafe and hanging tiny paper pumpkin lanterns everywhere. A barbecue with a rounded bottom had been wheeled in and disguised as a cauldron. "It's depressing in here," one of the customers had apparently complained.

"Don't worry," I said to Mum when she told me. "Depressing's good."

My contribution was to clean the chocolate stains off the bee costume I'd borrowed from my cousin Hadia. Dad's not keen on the whole witches and wizards thing, but dressing as a bee is fine. And like Dad said, bees are an endangered species and you don't get scarier than that!

I had dared to become excited. Perhaps this

party would turn out to be the one thing Dad arranged for the team that everyone remembered for all the right reasons. Fingers and antennae crossed!

9

On Saturday morning, I woke up feeling faintly sick but not mega bad. Then again it was only eight o'clock and the Queenies were not early risers. I kept my eyes on my costume the whole time I was getting dressed, so I could think about bees instead of Belles. Megan would not have been impressed, but if it helped, it helped, right?

"One plait or two?" Mum asked, waiting for me in the hallway, comb in hand, as I trundled down the stairs.

"I'll go with the one again, please, but go easy on the torture."

"As madam wishes." Mum smiled.

We chatted about the party. I think Mum was as excited about it as I was. "What about vegetarians? Any of those on the team? I'm thinking cheese and chutney wraps for them."

"I'm not sure. I think Katie might be," I said.

"Katie. Which position does she play?"

"Mum, she's the assistant coach."

"Oh, of course... I get muddled with all the names."

Dad bustled past, tapping his finger on his watch. "Hurry, hurry. It's late."

"Is it?" I asked.

"No, it isn't," Mum said. "Ignore him. He's been like a wired cat all morning." She turned to him. "What time do you think you'll be back? You still need to cordon off the grotto area properly and put the winter pansies outside the gift shop. I'll get one of the staff to—"

Dad cut her off mid-sentence. "Karmjeet, dearest. All that can wait until later. I've got other things to think about," he said briskly, grabbing me by the elbow the second Mum had fastened my hair bobble.

I glanced at the clock. Quarter to nine. "Calm down, Dad – we've got stacks of time."

"I have to be there early. I need to chat to Hannah."

"What about?"

He took a deep breath, looked at me, looked down at his feet, looked at the wall behind my head, then finally looked at me again. "The fog machine for tonight," he said.

"The fog machine?"

"Yes. I want to double-check whether Hannah thinks it's OK to use it." He paused. "It occurred to me that the twins might be scared."

I gawped at him. "The twins? Dad, they pluck their own chickens and feed live grubs to birds! They're not going to be scared of a bit of dry ice round their feet."

"Nevertheless," he said, "better safe than sorry."

"That's true," Mum said, reaching for her work fleece. "You can never be too careful. The health and safety brigade are so particular these days. They want certificates for this and risk assessments for that. Crazy."

"Crazy," Dad repeated brightly.

Mum gave me a tight hug. "Right, I'm off. See you both later. Good luck, Tabinda. Enjoy the match."

"Thanks," I said, my pulse quickening.

"And you, chill out," she told Dad, giving him a kiss and a pat on the cheek. "Save some of that energy for the party."

I could tell from his absent nod that he'd be ignoring that advice.

10

For once, Dad was quiet in the car. He barely spoke at all as we headed out of town and along the country roads towards Lornton. "It'll be fine about the fog machine, I'm sure," I told him, thinking he must have been worrying about that.

He didn't reply, so I gazed out of the window. The weather was the total opposite of last week's. The sky was already a cloud-free blue. The sun was shining, making all the trees and hedges, with their autumnal reds, oranges and bronzes, look even more stunning. "Typical of the Belles to get the best weather," I muttered.

Dad heard me this time and laughed. "The Belles aren't successful because of the weather, Binda. They're successful because they're well coached."

"I suppose."

"You don't win the cup and league five years in a row without good coaching."

"Mmm."

"The Belles are a team the Parrs should emulate."

"We don't want to emulate them. They're totally up themselves," I huffed.

"They're confident. There's nothing wrong with that."

The first Queenie arrived when he said that, quickly followed by another and another, like noisy passengers disembarking from a train. "I take it you won't be expecting me to score sixteen goals today, then?" I said.

"Scoring doesn't matter," he replied, sounding very serious. "Just show the same initiative you showed last week."

I shuddered. Showing the same initiative meant the same thing occurring: a high ball aiming to flatten my face like a chapati. I breathed out hard. Please don't let me have to use the same initiative, I thought.

☆ ☆ ☆

Despite the early start, we weren't the first ones at the ground. Megan, Petra and JJ had already arrived and Eve's mum pulled up at the same time as us. Eve, Amy and Gemma all spilled out of her car.

"I'll leave you to it, then," Dad said, and tanked off across the field to where Katie and Hannah were assembling the goalposts.

I joined my team-mates. Megan had already reached the pacing stage. She was walking to and fro, with Petra following her. "This is where it all starts to go pear-shaped," she mumbled. "You wait. Bend it like Becky's going to put six past me."

Bend it like Becky is really plain old Becky, but we call her that because it's what her fan club shout at her from the sidelines. She is a pretty decent player. OK, she's brilliant. We hate her!

"No chance," Petra told Megan. "Not six."

"No way," Eve agreed. "Maybe four or five. Not *six*."

"Don't joke, Eve!" Megan begged. "I'll be gutted if they thrash us again."

From behind us, JJ snorted. "I don't know what you lot always get so hyped up over the Belles for – they're nothing special. Just treat them the same as everybody else."

I glanced at her, watching as she flicked a tennis ball from one foot to the other, oblivious to everything around her. How could she be so laid back? So unfazed by anything?

"Red alert, everyone. They're here!" Petra announced.

We all turned to see a minibus pulling up in the visitors' parking bay that butted right up to the bottle bank. First off the bus was their hard-faced coach. Then one by one the Grove Belles descended, each one looking cooler than the last. As they trooped past us without a glance, I looked out for Bend it like Becky, but I couldn't see her. The other striker, a tall brown-haired girl who always ran circles round me, didn't seem to be there either. Nor their imposing goalie. Were they all injured or something?

Katie jogged across to begin the warm-ups. Hannah, amazingly, was still talking to my dad. Who'd have thought discussing whether to have a fog machine or not would be so time consuming?

"Who's reffing?" Megan asked, getting down to business. Her voice was calm and brisk. This was the point at which her nervousness left her. Lucky thing.

"That'd be little old me," Katie said. "So I expect your best behaviour."

"Sorry, but we will be testing you to your limits!" Petra teased.

"Cheers, Wardy. I love you too!" Katie laughed, then led the way down the side of the field. "Come on, Parrs. Let's see what you've got," she called over her shoulder. My stomach tautened as all the Queenies took that as a personal instruction to them.

11

A minute before kick-off Hannah chose the starting seven. I was twisting from side to side and bouncing up and down to distract the Queenies as she began to call out our names.

"Woah! Calm down, Tabs – you're making me feel seasick." Lucy laughed.

"Just want to get going," I lied.

"And which position would you like to get going in?" Hannah asked.

I turned to her. What a funny question – almost as though she was letting me choose. "Oh, anywhere. I don't mind," I said shyly.

"Then I'd better have you at the back with Holly, seeing as you 'excel' in that position."

Something about the way she said "excel" caught me out. She sounded – well, she sounded *sarcastic*. Hannah was never sarcastic. Ever.

"Is it just me or did Hannah seem like she was in a mood?" I asked Holly and Megan as we walked across the field to take up our starting positions.

"Hannah's *never* in a mood," Megan said, touching her bandana that was a replica of the one Hannah – her idol – always wore.

"Just my imagination, then," I said, looking for Dad. He was busy talking to the Belles' coach on the other side of the pitch. It wasn't unusual for him to do that; just stride over and strike up a conversation with the opposition – sometimes he recognized a customer, other times he said it was his job as sponsor to welcome people to the ground. It never occurred to me that today there might be another reason.

Katie held her hand up to check we were ready. The sun shone down on the field, like floodlights on a stage. Let the drama begin.

The first half was wild. First we had possession, then they did, then we did, then they did. There were throw-ins and corners and tackles galore. Megan was brilliant in goal, diving and using her arms, elbows, feet, knees, nose – anything – to keep the ball out of the net. At the other end, their goalie matched her, foiling Gemma and Eve every time they came close to scoring. I managed to intercept quite a few passes intended for their central midfielder, side-footing them out of play to safety.

"Well in, Binda!" I heard Dad shout.

At half-time we were still 0–0.

"I don't believe it. We've kept a clean sheet against the Belles!" Holly whooped.

"So far," Megan replied, picking bits of grass out of her ears.

"Awesome. Absolutely awesome. All of you," Hannah congratulated.

I grinned along with everyone else, feeling I'd done my part but happy to rest in the next half and watch. Surprisingly, Hannah kept me on, and in the same defensive position. The Queenies, who had been about to pack up and go home for a cup of tea, turned around again when she swapped Lucy in for Holly instead.

The second half began at the same breakneck pace. It was as if some unwritten pact had been made that both sides would give it their all. My heart was pounding in my chest, but I was actually enjoying myself. Most of the play had been on the ground instead of up in the air like it is when teams wallop it any old how. Then the Belles got a free kick just outside their area. "Push up!" their coach instructed, making a sweeping motion with her arms.

"Get back and defend, everyone," Hannah told us.

I did as I was told and ran to stand near the goalmouth, along with Lucy and three other Belles. My nerves went into overdrive. We were deep into header territory here.

"Watch the back post, Tabs," Megan warned me. "You might need to jump for this one."

I stiffened. That instruction had sounded eerily like the one in my nightmare. Well, so what if it did? I told myself. You can always run forward like you did last week. My shoulders lifted. I could, I thought. I could and if I had to, I would. Except that there was a post on one side of me and two white shirts in front of me this time, pinning me in. I had nowhere to run.

My heart wasn't just pounding now, it was clattering against my ribcage like a terrified, trapped bird. I sensed movement as the free kick was taken.

"Yours, Tabs!" Megan ordered, and that's when I totally bottled it. In panic, I shoved the nearest Belle so hard in the back she stumbled and fell forward. The ball, meanwhile, sailed harmlessly way above mine and everybody else's heads.

"Refe-*ree*!" I heard someone call out angrily just as Katie blew her whistle.

There was absolute silence for a few seconds. As in my nightmare, space seemed to miraculously open up in front of me, only this time, coming to stand in my eye-line was a disappointed-looking Katie. "Penalty," she said quietly, pointing to the spot.

I stood there, unable to move. I'd given away a penalty! Me. Meek and mild Tabinda Shah. Even Jenny-Jane had never given away a penalty.

"You take it, Mujgana," the Grove coach immediately instructed their centre midfielder from the touchline. "Keep it simple, like Becky used to."

"Budge then, Tabs!" Megan ordered, because I was still standing by the back post.

In a daze, I moved away. I couldn't watch as the penalty was taken. I stared at the grass until it blurred into a greeny mush, my head hanging in shame as I waited in dread for the triumphant yells. But they didn't come. Instead, I heard a groan and Megan shouting "Yes!"

I looked up, and Megan, Petra and Lucy were

bouncing up and down and hugging each other. Megan had saved it. Unbelievable!

Play resumed. Megan kicked the ball fiercely, lofting it perfectly for JJ to bring under control and push forward. JJ ran like she was being chased by hungry wolves, clearly determined that no one would catch her.

"Come on, Parrs!" Megan yelled. *"Come on!"*

JJ looked up, passed neatly to Gemma, who crossed to Eve, who had a shot. The ball narrowly missed, glancing off the post instead.

"Brilliant play!" Megan cried, clapping her hands together. "And again!"

The air crackled with energy as six Parrs responded to her rallying cry. The seventh went to pieces. I didn't run for the ball. I didn't even try to mark up. I just kept reliving the moment I'd pushed the Belles attacker in the back. When Hannah made a rolling motion with her arms a minute later, I almost cried with relief, but she didn't mean me. She took JJ off instead, and brought Nika on.

I kept going from hot to cold, from stiff-limbed to jelly-legged. The Queenies were having the time of their lives. They battered the walls of my stomach, like soldiers besieging a castle. After another five minutes I knew I'd be sick if Hannah left me on much longer. I just knew it.

As if to put me out of my misery, Nika scored with a thundering volley. It was fantastic, but instead of running to congratulate her, I bolted in the opposite direction. "You've got to take me off!" I said to Hannah, shaking and clutching my stomach. "I'm going to puke."

Her face was full of concern, and the coolness that had been in her voice earlier totally disappeared. "Of course," she said, and told Amy to get ready.

"What!" JJ said rudely, desperate to get on again. "*Her* instead of *me*?"

"Chillax, JJ." Amy sniffed, pulling up her socks so they were just so. "I don't know what you're getting so worked up for. It's only the Belles, remember."

Dad appeared then, his face ruddy from jogging across the field. "What's wrong?" he asked, worried.

"I feel sick," I told him. I was bent double, clutching my knees, and sweat was pouring down my face.

"Ah," he said, patting my back, "that explains it." And he dashed off again.

I stared in disbelief as he strode off, back to the Grove Belles' side.

Hannah glanced down at me. "Are you OK? Do you want a sip of water or anything?"

"No," I said, shaking my head and standing upright. "Thank you."

I could feel the Queenies fading away. But if the nausea was leaving me, the shame wasn't. "I'm sorry," I murmured.

"Oh – good ball, Gemma!" Hannah said, then turned to me. "Sorry for what?"

I swallowed. "Giving away a penalty."

"Hmm. What was that about?" she asked.

I was so tempted to tell her – it would have been the perfect moment if JJ hadn't been in earshot. How do you admit to being scared of headers in front of someone who could wrestle Rottweilers?

"I don't know," I said, my eyes welling with tears.

"Hey, don't worry about it, Tabs," Hannah said, putting her arm round my shoulder. "It's just one of those things."

"Megan's going to hate me," I stammered.

"Megan? Give me a break. She saved a penalty against the Belles. Megan will love you for ever."

"She'd have killed you if she hadn't, though," JJ added.

I laughed and wiped my eyes with the back of my hand.

"That's better," Hannah said, letting go of my shoulder to clap as we scored again. *Again!* Against the Belles! It was Gemma this time – with a header, no less.

JJ tore up the touchline with the twins, all three making aeroplane shapes.

"Mmm. That'll give your dad something to think about, won't it?" Hannah grinned.

"What do you mean?" I asked.

"He might change his mind about you going over to that lot."

"Sorry?"

She looked at me, and her face turned scarlet. "You didn't know...?" Her voice petered off and she cleared her throat a couple of times – the way people do when they realize they've said more than they should have.

"Know what? What do you...?" I began, then stopped. I looked across to the far side of the pitch, where Dad was trying to catch the Belles' coach's attention. I bit the inside of my lip. Of course! How could I have been so thick as to fall for the fog-machine line? Dad hadn't phoned a centre of excellence. He'd phoned our biggest rivals instead!

"Is that why you kept me on for so long?" I asked Hannah.

Hannah shrugged. "I wanted to give you every chance to shine," she explained, with a catch in her voice.

From the corner of my eye, I saw Dad striding across the field towards me. Inside my stomach, the Queenies, rudely awoken, were packing their bags and frantically calling out to each other. "Mayday! Mayday! She's going to blow! Evacuate! Evacuate!"

"I'm … I'm going to wait by the van," I told Hannah.

"Don't you want to watch the rest of the match?" she asked.

"No… I … I still feel sick," I lied, heading towards the car park.

"Feel better for tonight," she called after me.

12

"Hey. How are you doing?" Dad asked when he joined me in the car park.

I couldn't reply. I felt like a shaken can of Coke, tab pulled and ready to erupt. "Do you need a carrier bag or something?"

"No," I mumbled, sliding into the seat as he held the van door open. I buckled my seat belt while he strode round to the driver's side. It took me a while because my hands were trembling so much.

"Let me know if you do need a bag or anything, won't you? I don't want the van messy and smelly."

"Don't talk to me," I snapped.

"Excuse me?"

"I said, don't talk to me." I began shaking harder. Back-chatting my dad didn't come naturally. My parents aren't as strict as some, but I had been brought up to be respectful. I'd never been so rude before. "How could you, Dad? How could you tell Hannah I wanted to play for the Grove Belles?"

"Hey, calm down," Dad said. He reached out his hand, but I batted it away. His eyebrows almost hit the van roof in shock.

"You're horrible!" I added for good measure.

"Now hang on, Binda. I was just testing the water, that's all," he blustered.

"I don't want you to 'test the water'. I don't want you to *test* anything."

"But I have to. If I don't, how will you improve? Hannah's very sweet and all that, but she'd be the first to admit she's not an experienced coach. She only coaches the team for a bit of fun."

"I know! That's why I enjoy it! There's no pressure."

"Well, if you think you can get through life without pressure, think again."

"I'm not talking about life, I'm talking about football."

"So am I. Football is life to many people."

"Not at my age."

"Are you kidding? At any age! Haven't you heard those parents on the touchline? The things they shout out? Are you telling me they're not taking it seriously just because you're only nine and ten years old?"

"No, but..."

"And are you telling me that Megan and the others aren't taking it seriously?"

"No, but..."

"So it's just you that isn't taking it seriously?"

"No..." I said, my head pounding. Dad always did this: twisted things so I got confused.

He yanked his seat belt on. "I hope you aren't telling me I have been wasting all my time, energy and money on the Parrs when in fact I could just have taken you down the park with your cousins every weekend for a kickabout instead."

"No, no way. I do take it seriously; it's just that..."

But he pounced again before I could finish.

"Good. Now we're getting somewhere. You do take football seriously, so that means you are keen to up your game, right?"

"Yes."

"And I'm sure you'll admit at the moment you aren't doing that because you're inconsistent. Brilliant one minute, poor the next..."

"Only because—"

"Only because what?"

Like earlier with Hannah, this would have been the perfect opportunity to tell him about the headers. But as I drew in my breath and plucked up the courage, he came out with the very reason I hadn't told him before. "You see, you don't know. You don't have a clue, and that's precisely why you need coaching by someone with a bit more experience. Someone who isn't scared of making unpopular decisions. Someone like Layla Hodge." And with that, he started the engine, thinking he'd won me over with his argument.

I couldn't believe what he'd just said. Why did

he always blame Hannah? Why couldn't he see it was down to me and me alone? "Dad! Why don't you ever listen? I don't want to play for another team. I like it in the Parrs. I fit in. Not in a massive way, but in my own way. Like … like…" I fumbled around for something that would get through to him. My eye caught the sweet-pea motif on a stray business card lying on the dashboard. "…Like in a bunch of flowers."

Dad stopped the engine. "What?"

I twisted right round to face him so I could explain better. "Remember you showed me once how to put a bouquet of flowers together?"

He nodded.

"You put one expensive eye-catching flower in the centre, right, like a bird of paradise, or something?"

"Yes."

"OK, well, that's Gemma. She's the eye-catching bird of paradise."

"Go on."

"Then you add three or four varieties of something

not quite as unusual but still quality – like roses."

"Mmm."

"Well, that's Megan, Lucy, Nika and Eve. The roses. Then you stick in a couple of sprays of chrysanthemums, because they're hardy and long lasting – that's Holly and JJ..."

I was on a roll now, but Dad's smile had slipped, as if he'd guessed what I was going to say next. I carried on anyway. "Finally you add a few stalks of those tiny white bobbly things to pad out the whole bunch..."

"Gypsophila."

"That's it. Well, that's me. I'm the one who puts the 'filler' in gypsophila! No matter who trains me or how long I practise that's all I'll ever be."

Dad shook his head as if he couldn't believe what he was hearing. "What? You see yourself as a filler? My daughter? *Filler?*"

"Filler," I repeated. "Like it or lump it." I leaned forward and switched on the radio.

13

What I should have added was that even filler has its uses. That players like me and Petra and Amy weren't brilliant, but we were still part of the team. That we'd be missed if we weren't there. But I was wiped out from all the arguing and all the tension of the match. I think Dad was, too. We drove home, not in silence exactly, and not in a bad atmosphere, just … I don't know … in a strange kind of quiet, letting everything sink in.

Half an hour later, Dad pulled up outside the garden centre. The car park was almost full. "I'd better go and help out," he said.

"I'll get changed," I told him.

"OK. Mum'll be over shortly."

"Great." I nodded.

We parted with a clumsy, awkward hug.

I made my way home, round the path that ran along the front of the main building, across the field used for the camping display in summer and over to the gate leading to our house.

As soon as I let myself in, I headed straight upstairs, shrugged out of my kit and climbed into bed, pulling the duvet over my head. Going to bed at lunchtime was not my usual post-match activity and it definitely shouldn't have been that lunchtime, given the Halloween party, but it felt the right thing to do.

Duvets are magical, aren't they? Like a kind of protective shield. Nothing can get inside: no sounds, no bad stuff – nothing. Especially if you tuck all the corners round you like I did. I began to feel safe and cosy straight away, my head stopped throbbing and, unbelievably, I dozed off. The next thing I knew Mum was shaking me and saying, "Come on, lazybones, time to get ready."

"Ready for what?" I mumbled.

"Ready for what? Eyes rolling like bloodstained

marbles, of course." And without warning she peeled away the top corner of my duvet. Disaster! The magic seal was broken and all the day's events came tumbling back. The penalty, all the stuff with Dad and Hannah and Layla Whatsit. I let out a groan and tried to burrow back under, but Mum wasn't having any of it. "Oh no you don't!" she said and pulled me gently but firmly upright.

She was perched on the edge of my bed, an anxious expression on her face. "Are you OK?"

"Yes."

"Dad said you might be a bit upset."

I tried to sound chirpy. "Me? No, I'm fine. Raring to go."

She raised her eyebrows, but didn't ask me anything else. "Good," she said, standing up and unhooking my bee costume from the back of the door. She dropped it so it landed on my head. "Time to leave the hive, Clive!"

"Cheers, Mum," I said from somewhere beneath the heap of fur and polyester.

14

After I'd had a shower and bundled myself into the outfit, pulling it on over a brown polo neck jumper and thick black tights, I felt a bit more lively. Downstairs, Mum painted my face with some left-over theatre make-up my cousin had donated with the costume and straightened my antennae. She then left me to have some dhal soup while she got changed into her second-best salwar kameez.

"Oh, Mum! You look lovely," I said.

"I know." She beamed. "I thought the occasion called for a bit of sparkle."

Several of the assistants smiled at me as I passed them cashing up at the checkouts, but there was no sign of Dad. I didn't know whether to feel disappointed or relieved.

"Let's get cracking, then," Mum said as soon as we entered the cafe.

From then on I was – yes, I'm going to say it – as busy as a bee. I didn't have much choice. Mum kept passing me tray after tray of clingfilm-covered food to set out on the tables. "But, Mum, everybody's bringing stuff," I reminded her as yet another mini mountain of tuna and sweetcorn sandwiches was thrust under my nose.

"Last one," she promised. "Better too much than too little."

"You are so Indian!" I told her. "Food, food and more food."

"Don't knock it." She grinned. "Here, go stir these into the cauldron," she instructed and tossed a huge bag of chocolate eyeballs at me.

"Wow!" I said, peering into the cauldron and seeing for the first time what else was in there. Mountains of gruesome sweets: false teeth, jelly snakes, marshmallow fingers dripping in strawberry-flavoured blood. All miles tastier than the amaretti macaroons she'd set out for the grown-ups. I began to relax. Tonight wasn't about football. Tonight was about having fun.

The McNeils arrived at six o'clock, a whole hour early. The McNeils were never early! "Where do you want the ogre pus?" Mr McNeil asked my mum, his arms circled round a huge glass bowl of green jelly.

"Er … over there would be great," Mum said, trying not to look flustered and pointing to one of the tables that was already so laden with food only half a centimetre of tablecloth was showing.

"This all looks wonderful. Pity we can't stay," Mrs McNeil said. "We're going trick or treating with some of the boys' *ghoul* friends."

"*Ghoul* friends! Get it? Not *school* friends. *Ghoul* friends." Daisy chuckled, nudging my elbow.

"Clever," I said.

"Back round nine-ish," Mrs McNeil declared, then vanished, leaving Daisy and Dylan blinking up at me.

"Why have you come as a bumble-bee?" Dylan asked. "Bees aren't scary. Bees are nice – they only sting in case of emergency. Then they die."

"Because bees are endangered and nothing's scarier than that!" I said, repeating the reason Dad had given me.

"Mmm. That's more sad than scary, Tabinda," Daisy told me.

"Is that why you look sad?" Dylan asked.

"Pardon?"

"Your face says 'sunshine' but your eyes say 'heavy frost'."

"Don't be sad. It's Halloween," Daisy said.

"And we beat the Belles four–one," Dylan informed me.

"Did we?" I asked, my heart leaping, then falling all at once.

"Yes. In splendid fashion. Gemma did an upside-down kickle that highly flummoxed the ball-stopper."

"Cool," I said, slapping a smile on my face

and trying not to feel crushed for missing what sounded like a brilliant goal. "So, urm ... do you want to look round the shop?"

"Can we touch stuff?" Daisy asked.

"Sure."

"Golly! How splendid!"

They dashed off and I waddled after them. For a couple of minutes they bounced around like bargain hunters in the January sales before homing in on the Diwali candles and incense sticks. They'd just begun chanting spells over a brass incense burner when Nika's family arrived. More earlybirds! Nika was dressed as a witch: pointy hat, broom, striped socks – the works. She looked ... wicked. "My mum would like to know where we put the food," she said.

When I returned from showing Mrs Kozak the cafe, even more people had arrived and it was still only quarter past six. There were two vampires (Eve and Gemma), a mummy (Holly) and a grim reaper (Megan).

"Hi," I said to Megan.

"Hi," she replied.

"I … um … I hear we won."

She shrugged. "Yeah."

Her voice was so flat, I immediately assumed it was because of me going AWOL. "I'm sorry," I said. "Don't hate me."

She looked at me, her fake grey eyebrows meeting in the middle. "Hate you? What for?"

"Giving away the penalty and leaving early. I felt really sick."

"Don't worry about it. I'm not."

"Oh," I said. "I thought you might be cheesed off with me."

"No."

"It's just you seem a bit down … about winning."

"We didn't win, though, did we?" she grunted from somewhere beneath her scowl.

I felt confused. "But Dylan said we had."

Eve and Holly groaned. "Don't set her off, Tabs. She's going to start moaning about how winning four–one didn't really count because Bend it like Becky and that lot have all left," Holly explained.

"She only went over to their coach afterwards and asked where they were!" Eve continued.

"And their coach told her they'd all got too old for the team."

"Oh," I said, remembering Dad's similar prediction for the Parrs. So it had already happened to the Grove Belles.

"Bend it like Becky's at Leicester's centre of excellence." Megan sighed. "I'll never see her ugly face or save one of her hard shots again."

"There, there, petal," Eve said, patting her on the shoulder, "there'll be other Beckys."

"Yeah," Megan said glumly, "I suppose."

Petra and Lucy arrived soon after. Their outfits were harder to work out. Petra was wearing a huge belted raincoat, dark glasses and a trilby. "Skulduggery Pleasant," she told me after I'd guessed wrong six times. "Y'know. The book."

"Right."

"And I'm from another book. I'm Coraline's 'Other Mother'," Lucy explained. She looked the scariest yet, with her eyes painted like buttons and long, curved fake fingernails. "Remind me not to pick my nose." She laughed.

I dredged up a smile. It was impossible to remain miserable when everyone seemed to be having a good time. Megan was soon laughing at something Eve was telling her, and even JJ, who'd sauntered in with her hands in her jeans pockets and her England shirt hanging out, seemed to be making herself at home.

Hannah and Katie were almost last, arriving at ten to seven. They were evil fairies, their wings bent and broken, their teeth blacked out, their hair frizzed. It was weird seeing them without tracksuits, like when you bump into teachers doing their shopping at Sainsbury's.

But, of course, it was Amy who stole the show. Everyone stopped doing what they were doing and "ooh"ed when she made her grand entrance dressed as a jilted bride. Then we all laughed because she was walking exactly like a real bride coming down the aisle. She even had her mum carrying her train behind her.

At first, Amy looked like a normal bride in a long white dress, her Marge-Simpson-high wig covered by a full veil, but as she got closer, you noticed the little touches – like the veil was actually a bit grey and torn and the posy she was carrying was made up of dead carnations. But it was the dagger, surrounded by congealed jelly-like blood, sticking out of her back that was the real attention-grabber. Even Megan admitted she was impressed.

Meanwhile, in the cafe, Mum was having to find extra tables to put food on – Holly's cake alone took up half the counter – and Dad still hadn't put in an appearance. He *was* coming, wasn't he? I know we parted a little awkwardly earlier, but that didn't mean I wanted him to disappear altogether.

As if he'd been waiting to hear those thoughts, there was a crackling sound and the tannoy started up. "Is anybody out there?" Dad asked in an unconvincing spooky voice.

"Yeah!" Everyone laughed.

I swallowed. Please don't let him start going on about bargain begonias. At that moment, all the lights went out. Every single one. The whole garden centre was plunged into darkness.

"Oh dear," Dad said. "What's going on?"

Nobody panicked. In fact, people "ooh"ed and "arrh"ed as various bits of costumes glowed – the twins' ribs, Hannah and Katie's hair boppers and Amy's wig. Yes, her whole wig was glowing like a beacon. So this was why she'd wanted it uber dark. "Is it working? Is it working?" she asked. "It should be lit like the Statue of Liberty's torch!"

While everyone adjusted to the dark, someone grabbed my arm, making me jump. "Take this!" Mum's voice hissed as she pressed a real torch into my hand. "Switch it on."

I did as I was told. A beam shone feebly on the floor as Dad's voice continued. "Ah, ladies and gentlemen, we have light. Would the Parrs please follow my little moonbeam to the grotto while the parents make their way to Count Dracula's Coffee Bar."

"Follow the lanterns," Mum instructed.

"What lant—" Before I could finish, a string of tiny paper pumpkin lanterns lit up at my feet, like cinema lights leading you to your seat.

"Minty," I heard Petra say.

They did look minty. So did the cobweb-covered Christmas trees, their tiny lights twinkling on eerie branches outside the grotto's entrance. If you concentrated hard you could just about imagine you were in a real forest, especially when the fog began to spread like an evil mist from the grotto entrance.

"Now that *is* cool!" Lucy announced.

"I'm loving it!" Eve declared.

I felt a surge of pride dart through me.

Dad had worked really hard on this.

Inside the grotto, fairy lights had been woven between the spiders and bats on the trellis so we could all find seats without breaking our necks.

"Now what?" someone asked me. JJ, I think.

"I don't know," I said.

"Now we begin." Hannah laughed – a throaty cackle. "Everybody take one of these," she said and handed round tiny glass bowls with battery-operated lights inside.

We sat in a circle. I had Lucy on one side of me and Holly on the other.

"Anyone scared?" Katie asked.

"No," we chimed.

"Well, a bit," Petra admitted.

"Good. Because scary is what tonight's all about..."

15

“First I want to kick off by properly explaining the whole reason for this shindig,” Hannah began. “The thing is, when you play in a team, getting together away from the sport is as important as playing the sport. Those of you who came to the summer tournament know all about that, don’t you?”

I hadn’t gone on the summer tournament so I couldn’t join in with the “yes”es and nods.

“Also, although some of you know each other really well from school, for the three or four of you who don’t go to Mowborough, there’s a bit of an imbalance. I know that Holly sometimes feels a bit left out, don’t you, with living the furthest away?”

“Mmmff,” Holly replied as a bandage slipped over her nose.

"Now, if you were all on the senior team, what we'd do to bond is go down the Queen's Head for a few pints..."

"...of orange juice," Katie added quickly.

"Oh, yeah. Orange juice, lemonade, herbal tea..." Hannah laughed. "But we can't do that with you lot, so we thought we'd come here instead. OK? Y'all up for a bit of bonding?"

Everyone cheered.

"Right. The first thing we want you to do is sit next to the person you feel you know the least well on the team."

There was chaos then as everybody swapped places, stepping over trains and scythes and pitchforks. I was paired with Gemma, which was good because I didn't know her well at all, but bad because I'm in awe of her. Bird of paradise meets gypsophila twig!

When everyone had settled down, Hannah continued. "Now, without thinking too much about it, tell that person three things about yourself they couldn't possibly know."

"My favourite food is cornflake tart and custard, I am learning Punjabi and I love Fernando Torres," I gabbled.

"My favourite colour is blue, I am allergic to strawberries and I ... um ... am really lame at things like this!" Gemma gabbled back.

"Now swap with the person on your left!" Hannah ordered. "And tell them three different things."

I got Holly this time. Then Daisy the time after and Nika the time after that.

My head was spinning when Hannah finally called us to stop. "Now choose one thing you've learned about a team-mate that surprised you the most and share it with the rest of us."

I was really pleased when Gemma picked mine. She said she thought it was funny that I liked cornflake tart and custard with me being from India. "But I'm not from India," I told her, "I'm from Mowborough!"

People smiled at that – but the one that made everyone crack up was Dylan revealing that Eve loves trumping in the bath.

"Why am I not surprised?" Hannah laughed. "OK, are you all sitting next to someone different?"

More swapping and clambering. I turned to see JJ's face, long and solemn, looking back at me. Great.

16

"Now this time we're moving into Halloween territory," Hannah said. "I want you to tell the person next to you the one thing that scares you. Really, really scares you."

My heart stopped. Of all the things to ask us to do. I looked at JJ, waiting for her to go first – but I realized there was no point because JJ isn't scared of anything. "I'm scared of rats," I said, and instantly felt guilty for lying, but I wasn't going to confess my fear in front of her. If I couldn't tell Hannah or Dad I certainly couldn't tell Jenny-Jane Bayliss.

"Why?" she asked.

"Because they're dirty."

"Yeah," JJ said, "a lot of people think that. My mam hates 'em."

"Mmm," I said.

I was expecting an awkward pause, so it was a surprise when JJ lowered her eyes and mumbled something.

"Sorry. What?" I said, leaning closer.

"School. I'm scared of school," she muttered.

"School?" I repeated.

"Yeah. School. What? Are you deaf?"

"Sorry. Er ... what scares you about it?"

Her hand tightened round the glass bowl. "Everything," she admitted. "The way everybody looks at you when you walk in. The noise. The smell. Teachers. Kids. Assemblies. Dinner times. Everything."

"Wow! That's a long list! How do you get through the day?"

I genuinely wanted to know. I loved school and couldn't imagine being scared of any of those things. I even quite liked Miss Parkinson, our old Year-Three teacher who nobody else could stand.

JJ glanced up at me quickly, then went back

to staring into the bowl. "I don't know how I'll get through the day. It's my first one on Monday."

"Is it? What have you been doing since September, then?"

She shrugged. "Going somewhere else."

"Oh," I said, a bit confused, but I didn't like to ask what she meant. All I knew was that this was the longest conversation I'd ever had with her.

"Monday's at your gaff," she whispered.

"My gaff? You mean Mowborough Primary?" My voice came out in a high squeak, I was so taken aback.

She flinched. "All right – don't faint."

A minute ago I might have done. JJ wasn't exactly my favourite person in the world, but seeing her so uncomfortable made me want to help her. "But you'll be fine – you'll be in Mrs Keogh's class with me and Megan and Petra," I told her.

Instead of being reassured like I thought she would be, especially as she got on well with Megan, JJ began to shake. "That makes it worse."

"Why?"

"It just does. I'd rather not know anyone than have you three gawping at me when I walk in."

I knew she was anxious. Even in the dim light, her face was tight and closed off, as if her Queenies were preparing for take-off.

"We ... we would have gawped if you'd just walked in, but now we know you're coming, we'll..." I paused, wondering what to say next. "What should we do?" I asked her.

She shrugged. "Ignore me. Or at least don't make a big deal out of it."

"OK," I said, "I understand."

"You can talk to me at break."

"OK."

"But not during lessons."

"OK..." I stopped, suddenly conscious that everything around us had gone quiet. They must have finished their exchanges yonks before us.

"That was a long one!" Daisy exclaimed. "You must be scared of loads of things."

JJ stiffened.

"Yeah," I said quickly, "I am a bit of a wimp."

"Do you want to start then, 'wimp'?" Hannah joked.

"No," I said, not quite ready and guessing JJ wasn't either. "Can you ask someone else first?"

Hannah didn't miss a beat. "Sure. Who wants to start?"

"Let me," Amy volunteered. She began to reel off a list on the fingers of her white gloves. "Carrots with knobbly bits that look like warts – they're freaky. Being stuck in a lift. That's happened to me twice now and it's beyond gross, especially when you're surrounded by strangers with bad breath. Next come spiders and snakes, obviously..."

Spiders and snakes featured a lot. Petra, Gemma, Lucy and even Katie listed spiders. Megan's was dogs, because she'd been bitten by one; Holly's was walking past a certain house in her village where there'd once been a murder;

Eve's was crossing over motorway bridges. "I keep thinking the bridge will collapse..."

"School," JJ announced quickly when it came round to us.

People laughed and agreed, but nobody asked her why.

"Tabs?" Hannah prompted, moving straight on to me.

"I'm scared of ra..." I began, but couldn't quite finish the word. I tried again. "I'm scared of ra..."

"It's OK. Take your time," Hannah said gently.

I swallowed. Glanced round. Everyone was looking at me, sensing I was struggling, and their faces were willing me on. "I'm scared of ra..." I said again, wondering why I couldn't just come right out and say it. I mean, it wasn't even true.

Then, to my amazement, JJ reached over and put her hand over mine. Just for a second. Just to reassure me that it was OK; people would understand about the rats. JJ, the toughest, hardest girl on the team, was comforting *me.*

That touch was all I needed. I took a deep breath. “I’m scared of heading the ball,” I said.

Nothing happened on the outside. I wasn’t struck by lightning. The cold fog round my ankles didn’t turn to ice. Nobody fainted and nobody sniggered. Hannah simply nodded, then moved on to the next person, just as she had for JJ.

Inside though… Inside felt spectacular. More like Bonfire night than Halloween, with fireworks bursting in all directions. And most of the Queenies were cheering and sending each other text messages, saying, “Finally! She’s only gone and done it! Put the blooming kettle on. I’ll be home in five.”

There was still one Queenie, though, in the corner of my stomach, shaking its head as if to say, “It ain’t over yet, kiddo. It ain’t over yet…”

17

When we'd finished going round, Hannah congratulated us. "That was fantastic. Telling people what scares you takes a lot of courage and trust in each other. That's awesome. That's teamwork." She paused and smiled at us all. "I'm not saying it will make your fears disappear just like that," she said and snapped her fingers. "And from that list, Tabs' is about the only one I can help with – but getting fears out in the open is the first step..."

I winced at being singled out, but Hannah did it in such a matter-of-fact way that nobody even noticed. Just accepted that that's what she would do, as a football coach. The lone Queenie prodded me. "Now you ain't gotta worry about the rest of 'em thinking you're getting special treatment, right, kiddo?"

Right. I perked up. Right! But he still didn't budge. Just leaned against the wall of my tummy and folded his wings, waiting. I squirmed in my seat as Katie took over.

"Getting things out in the open is definitely the way to go," she said. "I remember a couple of years ago I had something I wanted to tell my mum and dad and I was really scared about how they'd react..."

I sat up, listening hard.

"...I spent months agonizing over when to tell them and what to say. I used to wake up at night in such a panic!"

That was me she was describing. Me exactly.

"Finally it just burst out of me one night. We were watching the draw for the National Lottery, and I just told them. There was a bit of a pause, and then my mum just shrugged and goes, 'Oh, we know that, ducky! We've known for ages.' And my dad went, 'You've made me miss the bonus ball now!' And that was it. End of! I'd been getting my knickers in a twist over something they already knew."

"That you were scared of spiders?" Daisy asked.

"Something like that!" Katie grinned and turned to Hannah.

Hannah leaned forward and waved her broken wand. "Right then, m'dearies. Time for a spooky challenge..."

I jumped up, fell back down again, because of the weight of my bee costume, and stood up again with the help of JJ and Nika. "Sorry," I said, as everybody laughed, "just remembered something. Back in a bit."

I had a spooky challenge of my own to do.

18

"Headers?" Dad exclaimed as we stood by the winter pansies between the cafe and the gift shop. "You're scared of headers?"

"Yes," I said, tilting my chin, ready to challenge him if he started on about how he could fix that little problem. "I am scared of headers."

"What are headers?" Mum asked.

Dad rolled his eyes. "Headers. Like it says on the tin. When you use your head to direct the ball."

"I get scared," I told her, the words flowing so easily now. "I get scared they'll smash me in the face."

"I'm not surprised. I would too," Mum said, licking some ogre pus from her finger. "Why do you have to head it, anyway? Why can't you just kick it?"

"That's what I've been asking myself." I grinned.

"Can't I just kick it? But you can't. Not every time."

"You're scared of headers, though? Seriously?" Dad asked.

"Yes," I said, "very seriously."

"Why didn't you tell me?"

"Because I knew you'd make a big deal about it and that would have made it worse."

"A big deal? No I wouldn't. I'd have—"

"Ali," Mum said, with a shake of her head. "There's a reason we have two ears and only one mouth. Listen, for once."

"I..." Dad began, then stopped. He cleared his throat. "You're right," he admitted. "I would have made a fuss."

He looked so bewildered and crestfallen, I felt sorry for him. "Hey," I said, to cheer him up, "you never know. If I overcome my fear, I might turn into a rose."

"You'll never be a rose," he said.

"Well, I won't be a bird of paradise, if that's what you're thinking!" I warned.

"Why would I want you to be either?" Dad asked. "You know you are my sweet pea!"

"His favourite flower," Mum reminded me.

I wrapped my arms round him and gave him a hug, or as much of a hug as I could manage with a fat spongy tummy. He kissed the top of my furry bonce. "My Binda. Scared of headers," he said. "Poor baby."

I pushed him away. "Poor baby? Urgh! That's it! This is getting too gushy now. If you don't mind, I am going to return to the vampires and other freaks."

"Good idea. And while you're there, can you ask how long you freaks will be?" Mum asked. "Only the ogre pus is looking a bit septic."

"I don't think we'll be that long," I said, with a huge beam on my face. "We're pretty much there on the team-building thing."

Final Whistle

I wish I could tell you that since that night I went on to score goal after goal with my awesome, diving headers. But I'm afraid not. It isn't that easy to get over a real fear. I'm taking it sloooooooooooowly.

Hannah's helped me loads. She started by telling me that it didn't matter one bit if I got to the end of the season without once heading the ball. I could just keep doing what I've been doing. And just knowing that stopped me being such a worry wart.

The first step, when I'm ready, is for someone to gently bounce a sponge ball against my forehead, and for me to nudge it away. I'm thinking of asking JJ. We could do it at lunchtimes, somewhere quiet. Or maybe Dad. He's been so subdued by missing all signs of my headerphobia – if I gave any – that he hardly comments about my football any more. He's stopped criticizing Hannah, too. I think he's realized that even if she hasn't got loads of experience or qualifications she still knocks spots off anyone else. Besides, it's the Parrs who are still at the top of the table! And you can't argue with that, can you.

It's Gemma, the bird of paradise, who follows on from here, so I'll say goodbye now. Oh, and if you're ever near Mowborough and fancy a cup of tea and a scone, please drop by Sweet Peas Garden Centre. We'd love to see you!

Your friend,
Tabinda xxxx

The Nettie Honeyball Women's Football League junior division

Team	P	W	D	L	Pts
Parrs U11s	6	5	1	0	16
Furnston Diamonds	6	4	2	0	14
Tembridge Vixens	6	3	3	0	12
Grove Belles	6	3	2	1	11
Greenbow United Girls	6	3	1	2	10
Hixton Lees Juniors	6	2	1	3	7
Cuddlethorpe Tigers	6	1	1	4	4
Misslecott Goldstars	6	1	1	4	4
Lutton Ash Angels	6	1	0	5	3
Southfields Athletic	6	1	0	5	3